Books are to be
the last

Collins

Roaring Good Reads will fire the imagination of all young readers – from short stories for children just starting to read on their own, to first chapter books and short novels for confident readers.

www.roaringgoodreads.co.uk

Also by Vivian French

Morris the Mouse Hunter
Morris in the Apple Tree
Guinea Pigs on the Go
Guinea Pigs go to Sea

More Roaring Good Reads from Collins

The Littlest Dragon *by Margaret Ryan*
Spider McDrew *by Alan Durant*
Daisy May *by Jean Ure*
Witch-in-Training: Flying Lessons *by Maeve Friel*
Dazzling Danny *by Jean Ure*
The Elephant Child *by Mary Ellis*
King Henry VIII's Shoes *by Karen Wallace*
The Gargling Gorilla *by Margaret Mahy*
Mister Skip *by Michael Morpurgo*
The Witch-in-Training series *by Maeve Friel*

MORRIS
AND THE CAT FLAP

Vivian French

Illustrations by Olivia Villet

An imprint of HarperCollins*Publishers*

First published in Great Britain by CollinsChildren'sBooks in 1996
This edition published in Great Britain by Collins in 2002
Collins is an imprint of HarperCollins*Publishers* Ltd
77-85 Fulham Palace Road, Hammersmith, London W6 8JB

The HarperCollins*Children'sBooks* website address is
www.harpercollinschildrensbooks.co.uk

3 5 7 9 8 6 4

Text copyright © Vivian French 1996
Illustrations © Olivia Villet 2002

ISBN 0 00 714161 0

The author and illustrator assert the moral right to be
identified as the author and illustrator of the work.

Printed and bound in England by Clays Ltd, St Ives plc

For dearest Tricia,
with love

Chapter One

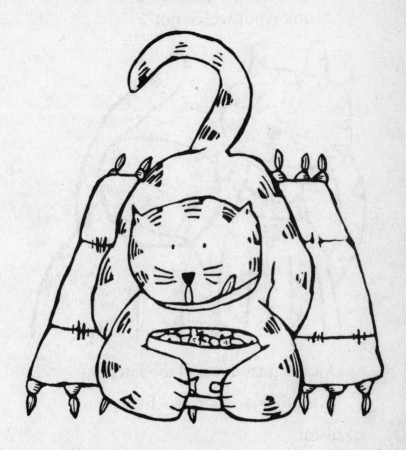

Morris was ginger and white and
very fat.

"Morris!" said his big sister Rose.
"Look what we've got!"

Morris gazed round the kitchen.

Everything looked much the same
as usual.

"What is it?" he asked.

Rose sighed. "Look at the door!"

Rose was right. Something very strange had happened to the back door. Morris sat in the middle of the kitchen floor and stared.

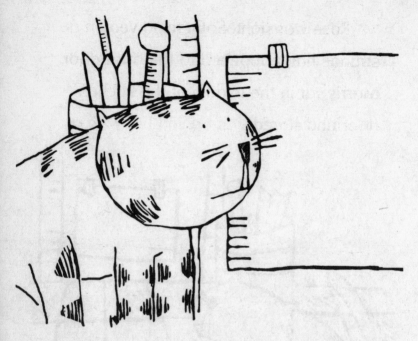

"What's it for?" he asked. "Why is there a window in the door? We've got windows already. Big ones."

"It's not a window," said Rose. "It's a cat flap."

"But what's it FOR?" Morris asked again.

"It's for us," said Rose. "We can go outside whenever we like." She bounced outside.

The cat flap shut behind her with a SNAP. Morris jumped.

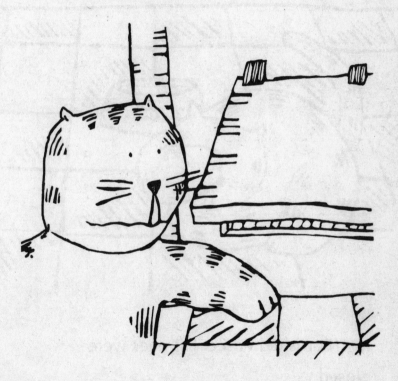

"And," said Rose as she bounced back, "we can come inside whenever we like. See?"

Morris didn't see. His eyes were closed.

"Why are you sitting with your eyes closed?" asked Rose.

"I'm waiting for the SNAP," said Morris.

"It won't hurt you," said Rose.

"Come and try!"

"No, thank you," said Morris.

"Suit yourself," said Rose, and she bounced out again.

Morris went to see if there was anything to eat.

Mother Cat yawned, stretched, and
sat up on the big chair.

"Morris," she said. "What are you doing?"

"Eating," said Morris.

His mother leapt down. "Has Rose shown you how to use the cat flap?"

Morris nodded. His mouth was full.

"Good," said his mother. "It's getting too cold to leave the window open all the time." She slid gracefully through the cat flap.

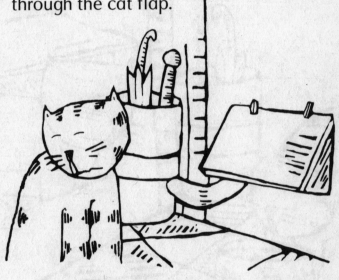

Morris shut his eyes and waited for the SNAP. Nothing happened, so he opened them again. His mother had disappeared.

"Morris!" Mother Cat's head was
pushing the flap open. "Come outside!"

Morris licked the last crumbs from
his bowl. "I'm busy," he said.

"Nonsense," said his mother. "You
need some fresh air."

Morris inspected the door. "I can't,"
he said. "The door's shut." He looked
up at the window. "And the window's
shut too."

"Use the cat flap!" said his mother.

Morris sat down. "I think I'll just clean my whiskers. You always tell us to clean our whiskers after eating."

"Hmm," said his mother, and she vanished.

Morris's little brother Tom came skipping in to the kitchen.

"Hello, Morris!" he said. "Have you seen our new door?"

"It's not a door," Morris said. "It's a flap. And it snaps."

"It doesn't snap at ME," Tom said,
and he skipped through it.

A moment later he peered back in.
"Did it snap?" he asked.

Morris went on cleaning his whiskers.

"I didn't notice," he said. "I'm busy."

"Come and play!" invited Tom.

"No thank you," Morris said. "I told you. I'm busy."

"You'll get fatter if you don't get any exercise," said Tom. He sniggered. "Too fat to go through the cat flap! You'll get stuck!"

"Go away!" said Morris.

Tom went.

Chapter Two

After Morris had cleaned his whiskers he
licked his paws. Then he walked slowly
and carefully to the cat flap. It didn't
look very big. In fact, the longer Morris
looked at it the smaller it seemed to be.
He stood and thought about it.

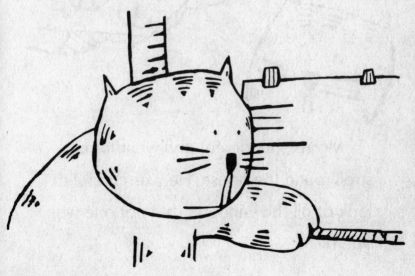

What if Tom was right? What if he was too fat?

What if he got stuck, half in and half out?

Morris shuddered, and went for a stroll round the house. He was careful to look at all the windows, but not one was open.

Morris began to feel uncomfortable.
He went back to the kitchen.

"Morris!" said Rose, appearing through
the cat flap like a jack-in-the-box.
"Come outside!"

Morris shook his head.

"You haven't been out all day!" said
Rose.

Morris shrugged.

Rose looked at him. "You're frightened!" she said. "You're frightened of going through the cat flap!"

"No I'm not!" said Morris.

"You think it'll snap on your tail and chop it off!" said Rose.

"No I don't," said Morris.

Rose yawned. "Oh well. It's nearly supper time."

Morris brightened. "Is it?"

"I'll see you soon," said Rose, and she jack-in-the-boxed out.

Morris waited until Rose had disappeared. He tiptoed to the cat flap and patted it. It swung to and fro before snapping shut. Morris sat down and thought about it.

What if Rose was right? What if it did snap on his tail? What if it chopped his beautiful tail right off?

Morris shivered, and went to sit by the front door. It stayed firmly shut.

Morris didn't eat as much supper as he usually did.

"Morris!" said his mother. "Are you all right?"

Tom skipped round Morris. "Morris didn't have any exercise. Morris is a fatty!"

"He hasn't been out all day!" said Rose.

Mother Cat looked worried.

"I'm quite all right!" said Morris.

"You'd better go to bed early," said Mother Cat.

Morris nodded. He was feeling very uncomfortable.

That night Morris had an accident.

"MORRIS!" said his mother, looking
at the little pool by the door.

Morris looked embarrassed. "I couldn't
find my way outside," he said. "The
window was shut."

Rose glared at him. "You're MUCH too old to have accidents," she said.

Morris drooped. "It was only a very little one."

Tom pranced up and pulled Morris's tail. "I NEVER have accidents," he boasted, "and I'm younger than you."

"Why didn't you use the cat flap?" asked his mother.

"I forgot," he said.

Rose sniffed loudly. "I think you're a big baby," she said. "And I don't think you deserve any breakfast!"

Morris went to sit in the corner of the kitchen.

Chapter Three

Mother Cat ate her breakfast and slid through the cat flap to see about a strange rustling under the tool shed.

Rose ate her breakfast and bounced through the cat flap to sharpen her claws on the garden fence.

Tom ate his breakfast and skipped through the cat flap to play with the butterflies under the apple tree.

Morris was all alone in the kitchen. For the first time in his life he didn't feel hungry. He heaved himself up on to the window ledge and looked out. It was a fine, sunny day. Morris sighed heavily. He wondered if he would ever be able to go outside again. Feeling extremely sorry for himself he curled up and went to sleep.

Morris was woken by the flapping of the curtains. He looked up in surprise.

THE WINDOW WAS OPEN!

With a loud MERRRUP! of delight Morris leapt outside.

The garden had never smelt so wonderful. Morris set off down the path purring loudly.

Tom was crouching by the apple
tree. He was staring at a large white
butterfly that was trying to make up its
mind whether to settle or not.

Morris arrived in a large furry heap.
The butterfly flew off.

"MORRIS!" said Tom. "I was just going to catch that butterfly!"

"I've come to play," Morris said.

Tom shook his head. "I don't want to play now." He stalked off towards the house.

"Oh," said Morris. "Then I'll play by myself."

Morris skipped up and down once or twice, but it wasn't much fun.

He hid behind the apple tree, but nothing came flying or fluttering past. He patted at a large and shiny beetle with his paw, but it turned round and gave him such a glare that Morris coughed and pretended that he was just stretching.

The beetle sniffed and disappeared down a hole.

Morris went to see what Rose was
doing.

"Can I sharpen my claws too?" he
asked.

"If you like," said Rose. "I've finished.
I'm going home for a snooze." And she
strolled away.

"Oh," said Morris. "Well, I'll sharpen
my claws on my own."

Morris scritched at the fence with his front claws. Then he sat down to have a look.

"Hmm," he said to himself. "They don't look any sharper. In fact, I think they look blunter. I wonder if I'm doing it right?"

Morris scritched with his back claws.
The fence wobbled, and Morris fell over.

"Bother," said Morris. He picked himself
up and stared crossly at the fence.

"I think," he decided, "it's the wrong sort of fence. It's the right sort of fence for Rose, but the wrong sort of fence for me. I'll go and tell Mother."

Mother was nowhere to be seen. Morris peered under the tool shed, but she wasn't there.

She wasn't curled up in the catmint.

She wasn't asleep in the seed boxes in the greenhouse.

"Meeeeow!" called Morris.

A robin hopped up on to the wall and chattered angrily, but there was no sign of Mother Cat.

"MEEEEEOW!"

There was still no answer. Morris sat down and dusted his whiskers.

Nobody seemed very pleased to see him at the moment – not even the robin. Maybe they were still cross about his accident. Morris sniffed. They were very mean. Besides, it wasn't his fault. Someone should have left the window open.

Chapter Four

Morris stopped thinking and sniffed. What was that? He sat bolt upright, his whiskers quivering.

FISH!

Morris galloped up the path to the house. He gathered himself for the spring up to the kitchen window, took a deep breath and jumped.

SPLATTTT!!!!!

Morris saw stars. Hundreds and hundreds of stars. Whirling and twirling around his head.

Twinkling. Sparkling.

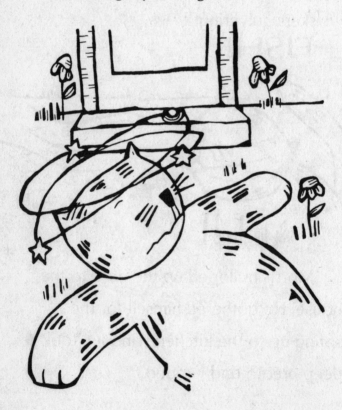

"Morris," said a voice in his ear, "Why didn't you use the cat flap?"

"He's too fat!" said another voice. "Morris is a fatty!"

And a third voice said, "Morris is frightened of the cat flap! That's why he had an accident!"

"Meeow!" said Morris feebly. "Meeeow, meeeow, meeeow!"

Mother Cat stood up. "Nonsense!"
she said. "Of COURSE Morris isn't
frightened of the cat flap. And he's
certainly not too fat! The very idea.
Morris, come here at once and show
Rose and Tom how you hop through the
cat flap."

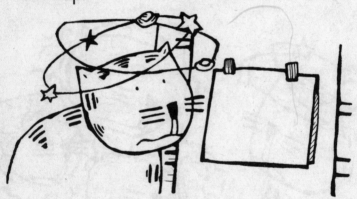

Morris looked at the back door. His
head was still spinning. The stars had
faded, but there were strange popping
noises in his ears. All he could see was

the cat flap. From this side it looked different. It looked like a little door. A special door. A cat-sized door that led to home and comfort and snoozes and – Morris sat up – FISH!

Without any hesitation at all Morris
hopped through the cat flap. Rose
bounced and Tom skipped after him.

Mother Cat heaved a sigh of relief
and followed them.

Morris was already half way through his fish when Rose said, "Morris! How did you get out into the garden this afternoon?"

Morris waved a paw. His mouth was too full to speak.

Mother Cat looked at him, and then looked at Rose. "I expect he hopped out through the cat flap. Didn't you, Morris?"

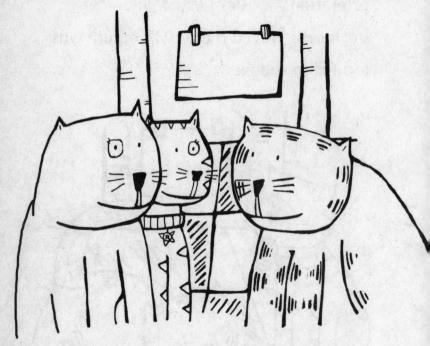

Morris stared at his mother. Did she wink at him? He was so surprised he choked on his fish and began to cough.

"There!" said Mother Cat. "You see? Morris can hop in AND out."

"Oh," said Rose. She looked sideways at Morris. "I'm sorry I said you were frightened."

Morris beamed.

"And me," said Tom. "I'm sorry I said you were too fat."

Morris purred loudly.

"So now," Mother Cat said, "Morris
will show you. Just watch him hop out
and in."

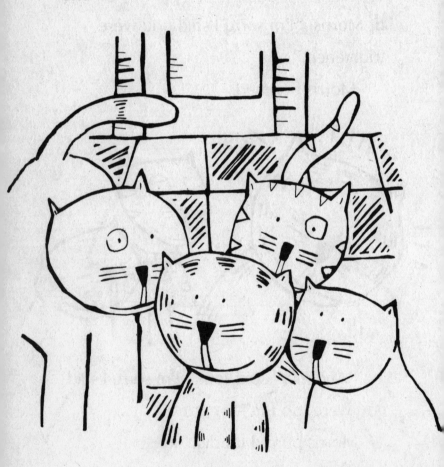

Morris gulped. He opened his mouth
to say he hadn't finished his fish, and
then closed it again.

Mother Cat was no longer winking
at him. She was glaring.

Morris took a deep breath. "Oops!" he said, and he hopped out and in the cat flap. Then, because he was more surprised than anyone at how easy it was, he did it again.

"Good boy, Morris," said Mother Cat.

"No problem!" said Morris, and
went back to eating his fish.